chook chook chook!

This is

_____'s

book.

OL' MAMA SQUIRREL

David Ezra Stein

NANCY PAULSEN BOOKS ◉ AN IMPRINT OF PENGUIN GROUP (USA) INC.

For Sam. "Chook, chook!"

NANCY PAULSEN BOOKS
A division of Penguin Young Readers Group.
Published by The Penguin Group. Penguin Group (USA) Inc., 375 Hudson Street, New York, NY 10014, U.S.A.
Penguin Group (Canada), 90 Eglinton Avenue East, Suite 700, Toronto, Ontario M4P 2Y3, Canada (a division of Pearson Penguin Canada Inc.).
Penguin Books Ltd, 80 Strand, London WC2R 0RL, England. Penguin Ireland, 25 St. Stephen's Green, Dublin 2, Ireland (a division of Penguin Books Ltd).
Penguin Group (Australia), 250 Camberwell Road, Camberwell, Victoria 3124, Australia (a division of Pearson Australia Group Pty Ltd).
Penguin Books India Pvt Ltd, 11 Community Centre, Panchsheel Park, New Delhi - 110 017, India.
Penguin Group (NZ), 67 Apollo Drive, Rosedale, Auckland 0632, New Zealand (a division of Pearson New Zealand Ltd). Penguin Books (South Africa) (Pty) Ltd,
24 Sturdee Avenue, Rosebank, Johannesburg 2196, South Africa. Penguin Books Ltd, Registered Offices: 80 Strand, London WC2R 0RL, England.

Published simultaneously in Canada. Manufactured in China by South China Printing Co. Ltd. Design by Ryan Thomann. Text set in Kane.
The black lines in "Ol' Mama Squirrel" were created with a pencil dipped into ink. The lines were copied onto Strathmore Aquarius II
watercolor paper, and watercolor and crayon were added. No squirrels were harmed in the making of this book.

Library of Congress Cataloging-in-Publication Data
Stein, David Ezra. Ol' Mama Squirrel / David Ezra Stein. p. cm.
Summary: Ol' Mama Squirrel has raised many babies and kept them all safe from predators, but she may have met her match
when a determined grizzly bear threatens to eat her entire family tree. [1. squirrels—Fiction. 2. Parental behavior in animals—Fiction.
3. Grizzly bear—Fiction. 4. Bears—Fiction. 5. Humorous stories.] I. Title. PZ7.S81790l 2013 [E]—dc23 2012021073
ISBN 978-0-399-25672-1
1 3 5 7 9 10 8 6 4 2

Ol' Mama Squirrel had raised many babies.
"Mark my words," she'd say. "There's no shortage of
creatures that would love to snack on a baby squirrel . . ."

". . . but it won't happen
on **my** watch!"

Whenever danger approached, Mama Squirrel went into action.

"Chook, chook, chook!" she'd say. "Get away from
my babies! Chook, chook, chook! Get out of my tree!"

No one could scold like Ol' Mama Squirrel.
The cat or owl that ran afoul of her would slink
off, looking for some easier meal.

One day, while the babies were taking a nap,
a nosy dog came sniffing around.

Mama Squirrel clattered
in the high branches.

chook
chook
chook!

She chattered in
the low branches.

chook chook
chook!

She scrabbled
right side up
and upside down
while she scolded
that dog.

chook chook
chook!

"This squirrel is crazy!" said the dog.
"They must put crazy powder in
the nuts around here! HELP!"

"And **that** takes care of that,"

said Ol' Mama Squirrel.

Mama Squirrel did not limit herself to known predators.

She scolded kites . . .

And airplanes . . .

She even scolded the man who came to prune the tree.

"And **that** takes care of that,"
said Ol' Mama Squirrel.

One afternoon, while the babies were having a scamper on a high branch, a great, growling grizzly bear came to town and climbed into Mama Squirrel's tree.

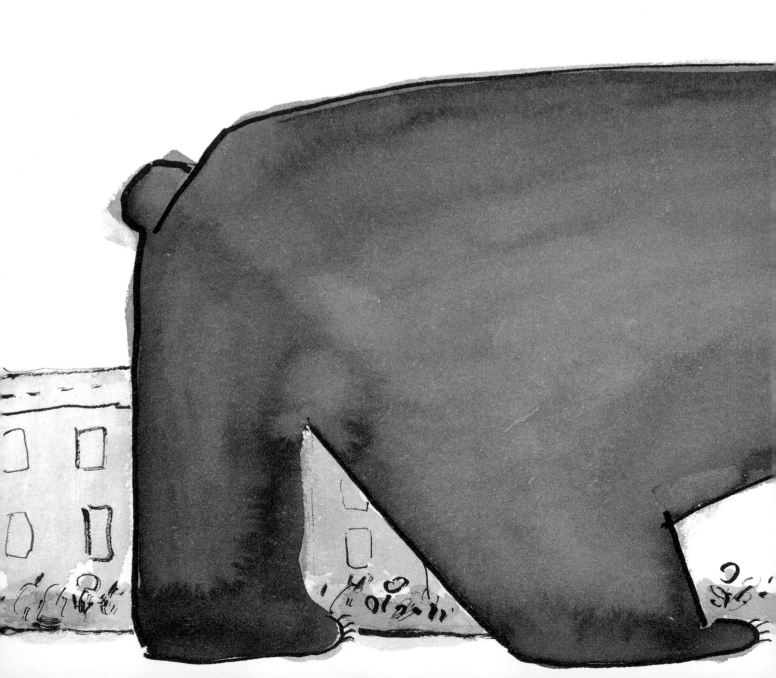

Mama Squirrel sprang into action.

chook Chook chook!

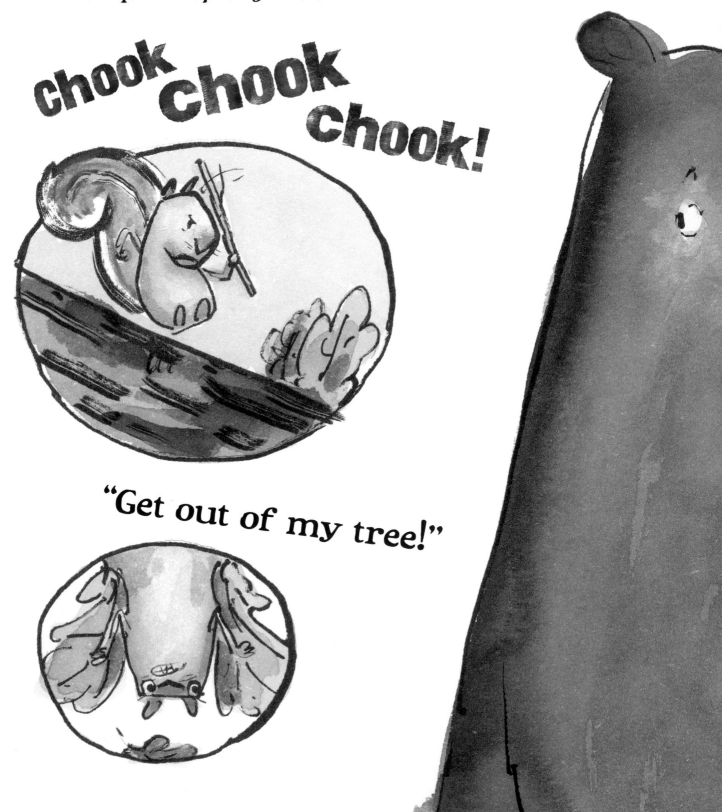

"Get out of my tree!"

chook
chook
chook!

"Get away from my babies!"

She clattered in the high branches and chattered
in the low branches as she scolded that bear . . .

. . . and she pelted him with last year's nuts.

PLONK!

The bear was shocked. But then he laughed.
"WA-HA-HA! Why should I listen to one puny
squirrel like you? I'll eat your whole family tree."

A twitch of fear went through Ol' Mama
Squirrel's whiskers.

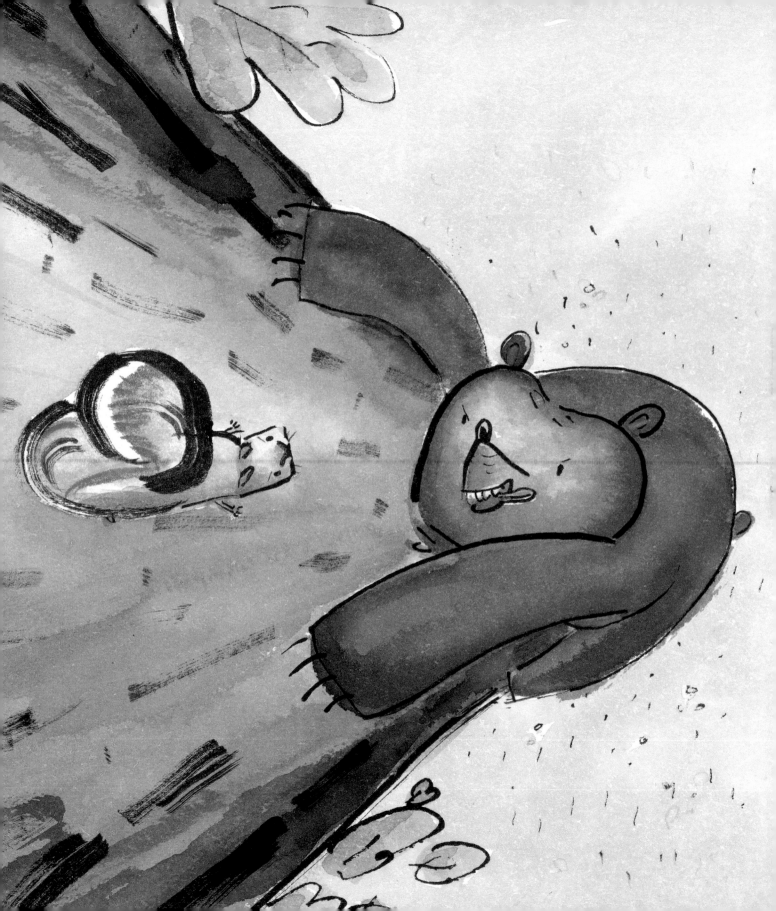

But then she clenched her jaw.

"Not on **my** watch, buster!" said Ol' Mama Squirrel.
She scooped up her babies and went to raise the alarm.

chook chook chook!

By the fire escape.

chook chook chook!

Under the tracks.

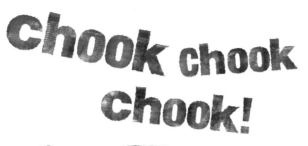

chook Chook chook!

In the tops of the trees.

Chook Chook Chook!

All over the park.

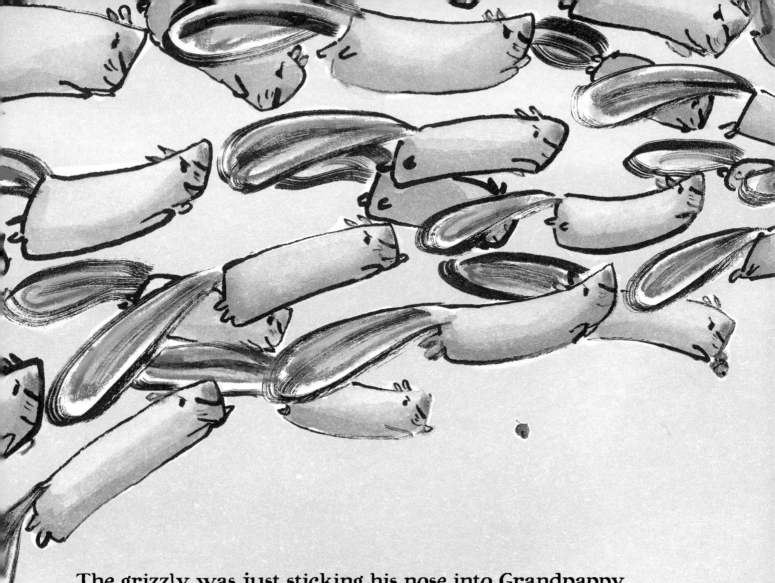

The grizzly was just sticking his nose into Grandpappy
Squirrel's nest hole when Ol' Mama Squirrel got back.

"Chook, chook, chook!" said Ol' Mama Squirrel.
"Chook, chook, chook!" said twenty other mama squirrels.
"Chook, chook, chook!" said one hundred more mama squirrels.

And they scolded him high and scolded him low
and threw old nuts at him

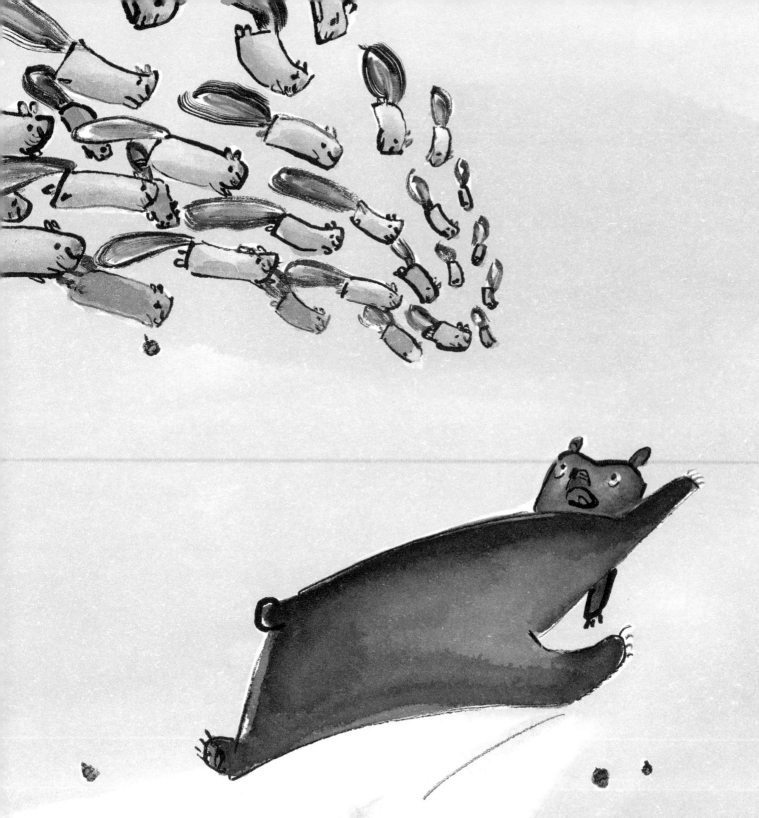

until he ran away and never came back.

"And **that** takes care of that,"
said Ol' Mama Squirrel.

The people of the town were grateful to
Ol' Mama Squirrel. They even put up a plaque
on the spot where she scolded the grizzly.

If you're ever in town, you should go see it . . .